This book is dedicated with love to my husband Lynn and to our son River and to ALL the rivers that carry life to the lands. This book is also dedicated, with big love and thanks, to the amazing Teddy, Emma and Jessika — folks at Medicine Wheel Education. They are a perfect circle of talent.

Editor: Emma Bullen
Text & illustration copyright © Medicine Wheel Education Inc. 2016
All rights reserved. Printed in PRC
ISBN- 978-0-9938694-4-0
For more book information go to www.medicinewheel.education

The Sharing Circle

Morning Star and River were two funny foxes who were the best of friends. They lived with the skunk, rabbits, deer, badger and buffalo on the Great Plains where the grasslands stretched out for miles under a never-ending sky.

Every day Morning Star, River and their friends played together in the grass. They hunted for bugs, swam in the creek and lay on their backs looking for shapes in the clouds. When the sun began to set, they all raced home to their cozy beds.

One day, while the animals splashed in the creek, River gave Morning Star a playful shove. Morning Star lost her footing and fell. She was so angry that she growled at River. They had a terrible fight, told each other "I don't want to be your friend anymore!" and crept back to their homes with hurt feelings.

The next day, the two foxes refused to talk to each other. It made everyone sad to see their friends fighting, and without their funny playmates, none of the other animals wanted to play. Everyone gossiped about the argument and began to pick sides.

When one of the older buffalos heard about it,
she knew that something must be done. She took a
braid of sweetgrass as a gift to a Great Horned owl,
called Kokom. The wise and mighty Kokom always
knew how to solve problems. She listened as the
kind buffalo told her the story.

"It is time we held a Sharing Circle," she said.

So the buffalo and the owl went down to the creek, and
all the animals gathered together to make one big circle.

"Many things we need for a good life are like a circle," said Kokom the owl.
"Water is one of them. What can you tell me about the water cycle?"

"There is water in the lakes and big oceans," said a smart young badger, "which evaporates and turns into clouds. The clouds make rain, and the rain shares itself with people, animals and trees. It travels into streams and creeks and makes its way back to the lakes and big oceans."

"Well done," said Kokom. "We need that circle of water to live. It is a sacred circle. "When something happens that may harm our community, we come together and form our own sacred circle. We call it a Sharing Circle."

"Why don't you tell everyone why we're here today?"
Kokom asked the buffalo woman.

"Morning Star and River have been arguing, and everyone has hurt feelings," said the buffalo. "Today we're going to share those feelings and talk about what happened."

The owl nodded. "That's right! Everyone has a place in the circle, and everyone should feel safe and respected in it. You can share by talking about your feelings, offering suggestions, or talking about how you can help. But you don't have to speak unless you want to."

The animals passed a talking stick to their left in the direction the sun travels. The foxes, the skunk, the rabbits, the deer, the badger and the buffalo took it in turns to hold the stick and speak. Some of them talked about their feelings, and some of them didn't, but they all felt a part of the Sharing Circle.

22

"I wanted to help, but Morning Star told me to leave her alone," said a young skunk named Smoky. "I tried to say sorry, but River wouldn't listen to me," said Morning Star. You called me bad names," said River, with tears in his eyes.

One of the rabbits started whispering to her friend, who stretched her front legs and looked around her as if she wanted to leave the circle. Kokom saw this and spread out a large wing to get their attention.

"My girls," said Kokom, "you can share your feelings when you hold the talking stick. But now you must sit still and listen. A Sharing Circle is a place of listening and respect. We need to be quiet until it's our turn and we are holding the stick. This time helps us listen, understand and often see things in a different way."

The animals passed the talking stick around the circle a few more times, and even the quiet deer who were shy in the beginning became brave when they saw how safe it was to share their feelings.

The more the animals talked, the more they came to understand that the argument was all a big misunderstanding.

"We should have listened to each other and respected one another," said River. Morning Star agreed. The two foxes were very happy to be friends again, and so were the other animals.

"You see, young ones, ever since we have lived in this land, ever since the water has flowed, we have always respected each other," said Kokom. "Every animal has a duty to care for another, and everyone has a job to do or a gift to share."

"Will we ever hold a Sharing Circle again?" asked Smoky, the skunk.

"Of course, Kokom told her. "Sharing Circles can be used in many ways.
The teachings of the circle have been practiced for a long time.
And if we continue to respect the teachings, they always will."

The animals all thanked Kokom and the gentle old Buffalo Woman for bringing them all together. Then they ran down to the creek to swim and play together beneath the enormous sky.

Conversation Starters:

How many different animals can you count in this book?

Can you find a woodpecker/hawk/prairie chicken?

What did the animals learn?

What could we use a Sharing Circle to talk about?

Plains Cree Animals and Their Phonetic Pronunciations:

Buffalo = Puskwa Moostos (pus-kwah moos-toes)

Deer = Upsimosis(up-see-mow-sis)

Duck = Sisip (see-seep)

Fox = Mahkesis (muck-sees)

Otter = Nikik (nig-ig)

Owl = Oohoo (oo-hoo)

Prairie chicken = Ahkisew (ahh-ki-sew)

Rabbit = Wapos (wah poose)

Skunk = Sikak (si-gawk)

About the Author:

Theresa "Corky" Larsen-Jonasson is a proud Cree/Danish Metis Elder with roots in Red Deer, Didsbury and Maskwacis First Nations. She lives her life according to the traditional indigenous teachings that saved her life. These teachings flow from her parents, her 93-year-old Kokom, Christine Joseph of Cochrane, aunties, uncles, as well as from the Goodstrikers, Williams and John Crier families, all of whom she loves immensely. Corky serves as a member of the National Collective of the Walking With Our Sisters missing and murdered indigenous women awareness movement and a proud member of Red Deer's Red Feather Women. She is also a member of the Urban Aboriginal Voices Women's Council and Red Deer Welcoming and Inclusive Communities Network.

A Book of Medicine Wheel Education

Books for ages 7-12 (available in English and French)

Educational lesson plans and posters available online!